V-Day Auction

EMMA BRAY

One

Victoria

I CAN FEEL my feet pounding the pavement through the thin soles of my shoes. I don't know if Lyle if still behind me or not, but I'm not even going to chance a look over my shoulder to find out.

Lyle is sceevy and creepy, and the way he looks at me has been putting a chill up my spine for years. He's the city's most notorious pimp, and as luck would have it, he also happens to be my landlord. Deep down, I think I was always afraid this day would come.

The day when I would find myself out of a job and unable to pay my rent.

The day when Lyle would ask for something *else* as payment.

I saw his eyes light up when he came by for the rent this month and I had to tell him I didn't have it yet. I asked him for an extension, but of course, he said no. He suggested I settle the matter of payment another way.

He wants my virginity as payment.

One boyfriend. I told one boyfriend, and now word is out on the street and there's danger for me around every corner.

I'm nineteen years old and still a virgin, and I only told that boyfriend because he'd been pressuring me to sleep with him, and I kept putting him off.

However, finding that out hadn't put him off. It had only seemed to make him more determined, so I broke up with him.

That was at least three years ago. I haven't dated anyone since his betrayal.

I don't have time for men anyway. I'm too busy trying to make ends meet.

I round the corner and run smack dab into something hard.

I'm propelled backward by the impact, and then I feel hands on my arms.

I panic as I look up, but then I realize the hands are steadying me.

They're the hands of the man I ran into.

And good lord, what a man.

He's huge. He towers over me, and even though he's wearing a suit, I can tell he's ripped. His chest is broad, and he exudes power.

My eyes travel up that broad, suit-covered chest, along a strong, clean-shaven jawline and up to the brightest pair of blue eyes I've ever seen in my life. They're piercing me with their intensity, and my breath catches. I vaguely take in his dark, stylishly disheveled, model-worthy hair before I shake my head to break myself out of whatever trance I seem to be in and chance a glance behind me.

I don't see Lyle, but that doesn't mean he isn't far behind. I need to make it to safety before he sees me.

"Sorry!" I fling at the stranger, startling him further as I break from his hold and take off down the street once more.

I need to hurry up and make it to old Agnes' place before Lyle figures out where I've gone.

Valentine

What in the holy hell?

My mind and body are still reeling from the literal impact that little fairy had on me.

I don't know who she is or where she came from, but when she smacked into me and then turned such fearful eyes up to me, every protective instinct within me roared to life.

Green eyes, long, chocolate waves of hair that seemed to dwarf her tiny frame. She was such a little thing, thin and petite.

And when I instinctively touched her arms to steady her, a jolt went through my system at the contact. She turned those wide emerald eyes up to me and her breath caught, those puffy, pink lips opening slightly.

She was the most beautiful fucking thing I've ever seen in my life.

And like an idiot, I stood there all slacked-jawed on the street and watched her run away from me.

By the time I got my wits back about me and made a motion to go after her, she was nowhere in sight.

Who was she running from? Is she is danger? The thought makes me want to roar. My eyes scan the perimeter, but I see no one who looks like they're in pursuit of anyone.

My chest feels tight at the thought that I let her slip away. I don't know why, but I feel like I'll die if I never see her again.

I run a troubled hand through my hair and blow out a breath.

Fuuuck.

I have all the resources available to a man, but how in the world am I ever going to find her? I have no name or anything to go off of.

My phone ringing breaks me out of my stupor.

I scowl when I see my business associate's name flashing across the screen.

"What is it now, Carmichael?" I snap at him as I pull the phone from my pocket and answer him, my eyes still scanning the streets.

"I can't make today. Something came up. We'll meet tomorrow instead," he tells me matter-of-factly.

I growl at him. "Fucking hell, man. It's always something with you." I'm about ready to walk away from this deal just to save myself the aggravation of having to deal with the fucker.

He just laughs good-naturedly like it's no big deal, which only serves to heighten my irritation further.

"I'll text you the address of where to meet me tomorrow," he says placatingly.

I pinch the bridge of my nose as I drag in a deep breath to try to control myself. "I swear to god, Carmichael, if you don't show tomorrow, the deal is off."

He waves away my concern. "Oh, you'll see me tomorrow. Don't get your balls all in a twist."

I growl again before hanging up on him, the disrespectful fuck, but the thing about Carmichael is he's got enough money to not give a shit. He's got even more than I do, and I'm not poor by any standards.

Before I can even register what I'm doing, my feet take off in the direction the little fairy ran off to. I don't know how long I walk, my eyes peeled for another glimpse of chocolate waves and green eyes.

But I never find them.

Two

Victoria

I CAN'T BELIEVE I'm doing this.

But Agnes is right. The source of all my problems goes back to my accursed virginity. For some reason, men lust after it. It makes me unsafe in the world I live in. I'm always on guard, dodging lascivious, lust-filled stares, scared someone is finally going to try to forcefully take my innocence.

Fuck that. I need money, and I might as well get something out of it.

"Girls like us don't have the luxury of waiting for Prince Charming," Agnes told me with sad eyes. She used to be a prostitute back in her day. I don't judge her for it. I know she only did what she had to do to get by, and Agnes is my only friend. "You might as well get some money for it instead of having it violently taken from you for free or giving it away to some loser who claims to love you and will just leave you once he gets what he wants."

I nodded, accepting her advice. Agnes has been around the block. She knows what's she talking about.

She told me the address of this place and how she'd heard through the grapevine that they would be having an auction.

The V-Day auction.

Apparently, it's an auction held on Valentine's Day, and I don't even have to tell you what they're auctioning off.

Women.

Oh, it's not a sex trafficking ring or anything. All of these women are here voluntarily. They're probably other girls down on their luck like me. Girls who could use the money and are willing to trade one night of their lives away for it.

But from how the owner's eyes had darn near bugged out of his head when he found out I was a virgin, I have a feeling they don't get many of us virgins.

Which means I will be a hot commodity.

And that's fine by me because if I'm going to do this, I want to make as much money as possible.

I might have decided to do this to keep some bastard like Lyle from taking my virginity. This might be my choice, but that still doesn't mean I'm not nervous as hell.

I'm a virgin, for Christ's sake. The most I've ever done is kiss a few boyfriends. I've never even let anyone touch me down there. Oh, I'm no prude. I've read some books from the library. I know what the sexual act entails. I know the basic mechanics of it, but I've never done it, and I'd be lying if I said I wasn't beyond nervous about it.

This has been the longest wait of my life. I've stood back here backstage and listened as every other woman has been auctioned off before me. None of them were announced as being virgins, so I guess that's why I'm being saved for last.

I'm the night's hot-ticket item for all the old pervs who dream of deflowering a virgin.

I try not to think of it. My stomach rolls with nerves. I just might be sick if I'd eaten anything today.

Instead, I've been waxed and groomed and styled all day—all courtesy of the auction. They wanted to make sure their prize mare was as attractive as possible for the bidders.

I pull the thin robe closer around me, as if it will do any good. It's gauzy and translucent to make sure the men can see the lacy white bra and panties underneath it. In fact, I think the robe was only added for aesthetic effect. It certainly does nothing to keep me warm or cover me.

"And now," a hush falls over the audience as the auctioneer's voice takes on a conspiratorial tone. My heart begins to beat faster in my chest. "Lush and ripe, a delicate piece of fruit never before sampled, young and just ready to be plucked," I can almost feel the sexual tension radiating from the audience all the way backstage. My hands and legs begin to tremble. Oh god, what if I'm making a huge mistake?

The money, I remind myself. Think of the money. Think of the financial freedom you'll finally have.

"Victoria!" the auctioneer bellows my name with a dramatic wave of his hand, signaling for me to make my entrance out onto the stage where I'll be critically assessed and then bid on.

I take in a shaky breath, and even though my legs feel like jelly, I somehow force them to carry me out into the bright lighting of the stage where at least a hundred pairs of hungry male eyes are suddenly on me.

Dear god, I suddenly pray, please let whoever buys me be somewhat kind. I'm silently praying that whoever gets me isn't a monster who will get off on inflicting pain on a virgin on her first time. I don't even care if it's a gross old man so long as he makes it quick and is somewhat gentle. I don't need someone who's into sick, kinky shit.

I try to stop myself, but I'm trembling from head to toe, and I can't help it. I chance a look out over the crowd, and if the lustful stares and licked lips are any indication, my fear might only be enhancing their desire. They're like a pack of wolves, and I'm the lamb set before them for slaughter.

Oh lord...what have I gotten myself into?

Valentine

My scowl has been permanently etched onto my face ever since I figured out just what this event is.

Damn fucking Carmichael. Only he would have the audacity to have me meet him at a place like this. The fucker probably did this on purpose. He's probably getting some sort of sadistic glee out of yanking me around like this.

Not only do I show up to what I find out is some

sort of flesh auction, but I can't find the asshole anywhere. There are too many men in attendance here.

I've searched the crowd high and low, and I'm just about fed up.

Fuck this, and fuck Carmichael. I'm getting the fuck out of here.

I turn and start making my way toward the exit when the auctioneer announces another pound of flesh up for sale. My lip curls in disgust as I take in all the lustful faces around me. Like these men can't have anyone they want with all the money they have? Of course, I guess that's the way of it for some guys. They get tired of getting anything they want, and they need to seek some sort of thrill to get pleasure. The taboo of the situation is probably what turns them on the most.

I shake my head and hurry my footsteps, sickened to be in their presence.

I heard the whispers of anticipation for the unveiling of the main event for the night.

The virgin.

Many of the faces around me are old and graying, and my stomach turns at the thought of these men bidding on an innocent young girl.

But that's none of my business. The way I understand it, all the girls up for auction tonight willingly signed up for this.

Still, I can't help but wonder what would make a woman so desperate she would sell herself off this way.

"Victoria!" the auctioneer bellows the name of the next girl.

A collective hush falls over every man in the room, and my footsteps falter at it. I feel an ominous prickle run up my spine, and I can't help it. I find myself turning back toward the stage as if an invisible string is pulling me.

All the blood drains out of my face, and I feel like I might pass out.

It's her.

The girl who literally ran into me on the street the other day.

Her big green eyes seem even bigger standing up on the stage. She looks like a deer caught in the headlights, her face pale, making the pink lushness of her lips stand out even more.

Her long, chocolate locks fall around her shoulders down to her waist. It's covering her breasts, but I can make out a bit of white fabric peeking through, so she at least has a bra on, thank God.

Her stomach is flat and dips in slightly at the waist before tapering down to gently rounded hips covered in a skimpy, lacy excuse for panties.

The see-through robe flutters around her thighs, and I swear I can see her trembling from way back here.

Victoria. Her name is Victoria.

She's the most sensually innocent, beautiful thing I've ever seen.

And I'm fucking furious.

Why the fuck is she standing up on that stage? Letting all these men ogle her like this?

Then, it suddenly hits me.

She's the virgin.

This girl who has haunted my dreams every single fucking night since she slammed into me on the street is the coveted virgin who's auctioning herself off to all these fuckers.

Out of the corner of my eye, I see men adjusting themselves in their pants, their erections obvious, and I have to fight from tearing their heads off.

My sudden jealousy and possessiveness is insane. It should startle me, but it doesn't. I just roll with it, accepting it for what it is.

Since that day I saw her on the street, she's been mine.

I've been searching for her, as uselessly as it may have been, and now fate has intervened once again.

She's right in front of me. A second chance.

Yet, fate is a bitch that my little fairy is standing

before a roomful of hungry wolves wearing next to nothing and about to auction her cherry off to the highest bidder.

I set my jaw and begin pushing my way through the crowd, striding toward the stage with purpose.

There is no way in hell I'm going to let her do this.

Victoria is mine.

Three

Victoria

AS MY EYES scan the crowd, I shrink back from all the lecherous looks I see on the men's faces.

Oh god, this wasn't a good idea.

Then, my eyes suddenly widen when I see one man pushing through the crowd and making his way purposefully up to the stage.

Oh my god.

It's *him*.

The man I ran into on the street.

His blue eyes are burning into me as he stalks right up onto the stage.

I'm frozen in place, helpless to move or do anything.

The auctioneer is sputtering in obvious astonishment. "Sir! You can't do this! You must—"

The blue-eyed stranger growls at him and silences him with a look before he grabs me and slings me over his shoulder caveman-style like I weigh little more than a rag doll.

I vaguely register the sound of hooting, hollering, and clapping as well as a chorus of murmurs of protest.

I'm too shocked to even resist.

Where did he come from? What is he doing?

Why do I feel inexplicably relieved to see him?

"Sir!" the auctioneer renews his case with more firmness to his voice this time. "You can't just take off with her. There are rules and procedures that must be followed. The bidding hasn't even begun. You can't just deprive other men of the opportunity at their fair shot."

"She's not for sale," he rumbles as he continues to stalk off the stage with me. I don't have a clue where he's taking me, but I find I don't really care so long as he's taking me off that dreadful stage.

It's almost comical the way the auctioneer is trailing along behind us, still sputtering. "But—but—"

Another man steps out of the shadows and blocks our way. He's almost as tall as the one whose shoulders I'm slung over, but he's fairer than him

"Valentine," his smooth voice addresses the man holding me. "Put the girl down, and I'm sure we can sort this out amicably enough."

The man holding me—Valentine—curses. "Fuck off, Carmichael. This doesn't concern you."

"Oh, but it does," the man says, widening his stance. "I'm the one who runs this little auction, so unhand the girl and let's talk sensibly."

I feel Valentine's muscles tense before he slides me down his front. I slide over every ridge of his rock hard muscles before he sets me on my feet before him. He's tall—so much taller than me. And big too. He smells of some sort of rich cologne, and it's intoxicating. My head begins to spin.

I crane my neck to look up at him, and the rest of the world seems to fall away.

There is nothing but his eyes burning at me like blue flames. His face is set into a deep frown, but his eyes seem concerned. For me?

I'm confused and not just a little shaky—especially when Valentine removes his suit coat and drapes it over my shoulders to help cover me.

The man who Valentine addressed as Carmichael seems to have a gleam in his eyes as they flick back and forth between Valentine and me. "Well, well, well," he clucks, "I see you have expensive tastes, my friend."

The man standing protectively by my side doesn't speak. He just sizes up the man in charge of the auction, his jawline hard. "She's not for sale," he finally grits out.

I hazard a glance over at him, but I don't dare argue with him. I suddenly don't want to be for sale. I realize this was all a mistake.

"She's signed a contract," Carmichael states matter-of-factly, "and as part of her contract, she is to be deflowered in one of the communal rooms where others can watch. Too many have already placed their bids to watch her lose her innocence."

"What?" I suddenly speak up in alarm and see all the men's eyes turn to me. I had no idea about any of that. None of that was mentioned to me when I signed the dotted line. I was merely told it was a legal matter when I signed my innocence away.

No one ever told me I'd be expected to let a bunch of people watch it happen.

Valentine takes in my shocked expression and scowls. "She obviously didn't know that, and she's not okay with it."

Carmichael shrugs. "It doesn't matter. She's signed a legally binding agreement. She will be sold to the highest bidder, and then she'll make good on her agreement in the communal room." His voice holds a hint of a threat in it as his cold eyes flick to me, and I take an unconscious step closer to Valentine as menacing-looking men in black suits suddenly surround us. They're obviously guards or enforcers or something, and I swallow, turning fearful eyes up at my strange champion.

These guys mean business, and I did agree to the deal. I never should have signed anything without reading it.

I'm going to have to go through with this one way or the other.

I see the reality of that settle over Valentine's face as well. He glances down at me and purses his lips, obviously conflicted.

"Of course," Carmichael goes on, "if you want her, I could waive the bidding in favor of a private deal, but I'm afraid deposits have already been put down on the viewing. That part is non-negotiable."

Valentine looks down at me with a torn expression. For some reason, this man seems to detest the idea of me being sold, but if he's so against this stuff, why is he even here? I chew on my lip nervously and release it when I see his eyes hone in on it, his nostrils flaring slightly.

"Victoria," he whispers my name, and the tortured way he utters it has my eyes snapping up to meet his. They're asking me a silent question, and I feel my heart hammering within my chest. How is it possible that I can communicate without words with this man I hardly know?

I know what he's asking me, and the fact that he's at least asking me is more than I ever expected to receive at an event like this, so I find myself nodding at him, a silent acquiescence.

Losing my virginity to this man, my odd savior, would be much better than any of the alternatives out there.

In fact, having him be the one to take me suddenly seems more right than anything else has ever felt in my entire life.

Four

Valentine

VICTORIA'S CHOCOLATE locks bounce prettily as she gives me the slightest nod of permission. My heart is about to beat out of my chest at the magnanimity of what I'm about to do.

I turn to Carmichael, "Done. What do you want?" I tell him, making no effort to disguise the hard note to my voice, although I suspect I already know what he wants...

I'm proved right when he answers with no hesitation, "The deal. I want it affirmed with a sixty-forty spilt." The sixty percent goes in his favor, I'm sure.

I grit my teeth. He's taking advantage of the situation, and we both know it, but I played my hand too early in my impatience. When I stomped up onto that stage and slung Victoria over my shoulder, it became blatantly obvious she was important to me.

And Carmichael is a master at sniffing out a weakness and exploiting it to the max.

This is no time for negotiation, though, so I stiffly nod my head, agreeing to his terms.

The underhanded, slimy fucking snake. He'd best enjoy this deal because I guaran-fucking-tee he'll never get another one out of me.

The victorious grin that overtakes Carmichael's face has me aching to punch his fucking face in.

I ball my fists together at my side to resist the very real urge to do just that.

"I need some time alone with her first," I bark out.

Carmichael raises his eyebrows before he shakes he head. "I'm afraid I can't do that. We can't chance you popping her cherry before the spectators get to see."

I grit my teeth in frustration. That wasn't my plan at all. I just wanted to talk to her first. Set her at ease. Explain. Hell, I don't know.

This whole situation is insane. Fucked up beyond measure. And I'm seething mad that there's not a fucking thing I can do about it. I'm strong, and I'm smart, but I'm not strong enough or smart enough to get us out of this situation with all these guards standing at attention like sentries.

I glance down at Victoria's tiny frame. Her little head is turned up, staring at me with wide, frightened eyes, and my heart wrenches within my chest. God, I want her, but I don't want her first time to be tainted like this.

With perverts watching on while I take her.

I take her hand gently and feel the tremble in it as we follow Carmichael to the supposed communal room.

I sag in relief when we get to the communal room. It's nothing like I envisioned. I don't even know why it's called a "communal" room because it's more like a voyeur's box.

We walk into a bedroom-type space. It's sparse yet luxurious with its red satin sheets and huge mattress. The entire perimeter of the room is made of glass – glass that I know are one-way windows. They'll allow the onlookers to see in, but from our side, they appear to be nothing but dark mirrors. We won't be able to see any of the spectators on the other side, and I'm strangely grateful for that. I hope it will make this experience easier for Victoria.

I feel her hand grip mine tightly, and I squeeze it back reassuringly in response.

"Enjoy your purchase," Carmichael says smugly before he closes the door with a resounding click.

My nostrils flare at another rush of anger, and my jaw ticks as I try to take deep, calming breaths. Were it not for the little angel standing in front of me I would plow down the door and beat Carmichael to a pulp — consequences be damned.

I don't even want to think of what would have happened to her had I not been here. I can't stomach the thought of one of those men out there with his hands on her virginal flesh, salivating over her. They'd probably get off on her fear. They'd probably hurt her.

As it is, I have a more pressing concern.

The little beauty in front of me.

"Victoria," I taste her name again, loving the way it rolls off my tongue. It suits her.

Her emerald eyes snap up to mine, just as captivating as the first time I saw them.

They're framed by thick, dark lashes. My god, she looks like a little doll. Too pretty to be real.

"Why are you here?" I ask her.

She looks away from me and shrugs, unwilling to answer me.

I try another tactic. "Okay, who were you running from the other day?"

Her eyes snap back up to mine. They're wide now and become haunted at the reminder.

I find myself clenching my hands into fists at the thought that someone was out to hurt her.

A sultry beat begins to play over the speakers hidden within the corners of the room, a silent signal for us to get the show on the road.

She looks up at me again, her inexperience and trepidation written all over her features.

She swallows nervously before she says, "I think we're supposed to get started."

I trail my eyes over her scantily clad figure and can't help getting hard at the sight of her. What man wouldn't?

I don't have an issue performing in front of others. That's not the problem. The problem is my insane possessiveness of this girl. I'm balking at the thought of any other man seeing her bared more than she already is.

My eyes trail back up to find hers. A sheen of tears is glistening in them, though she's trying hard not to show them.

Fuck. Her obvious distress rips my soul in half.

I can't help it. I step up to her and place my palms on either side of her face, cupping her cheeks. Her skin is soft as rose petals beneath my hands. She's so delicate, and I want nothing more than to protect her and keep her safe from everything—even me.

"I am not going to intentionally hurt you," I vow to

her while looking into her eyes, willing her to see the truth in my own eyes.

Her eyes search mine, and then she takes in a deep breath. My eyes snap to the gentle rise and fall of her pert little breasts, and I feel myself lengthen and harden even further.

I haven't even kissed her, and I'm already like a rod of steel of in my fucking pants.

Jesus.

"I know," she whispers. "I don't know how I know that, but I do," she admits, and a peace settles over me at having her trust.

"It's just you and me," I tell her as I gently stroke her cheek, captivated by her, inexplicably drawn to her. "Forget about everything else."

I'm still burning to know why she's here, why she is desperate enough to auction away her virginity, but now isn't the time or place to question her. There will be plenty of time for that later.

I slip my coat from her shoulders. It falls to the floor in a rustle of fabric, and she's just standing there in all her beauty, staring up at me compliantly, giving herself willingly to me.

Now, she's mine.

And mine alone.

Five

Victoria

I SEE the switch in him. The questions are still burning in his eyes, but there's now a purposeful look to his face.

This is going to happen.

I'm fixing to lose my virginity to this man.

When I signed up for this auction, I thought it would be a quick affair. I'd be auctioned off, have my virginity quickly taken, and then be on my merry way with my money.

I didn't think it would feel so monumental.

But standing before this impossibly tall, dark-hair

man with his piercing blue eyes, I feel like this is the moment my entire life has been leading up to.

This is the moment that's about to change everything.

The way he's looking at me...like he sees right inside to the core of my being...like he somehow knows *me*—the real me—is shaking me up.

I'm trembling but not with fear anymore.

No, I'm trembling with emotion. Emotion so raw it's practically pulsing out of me. His eyes are holding me spellbound, pulling everything out of me.

"God, you're so beautiful," he whispers as he lowers his head to mine.

I know he's going to kiss me, but I'm not prepared for the lightning that zips through me the moment his lips meet mine.

They press softly yet firmly against mine as his hands continue to gently frame my face. It's just the lightest press of his lips, and I feel like I'm on fire.

I wonder if he feels it too because he suddenly pulls me flush against him and deepens the kiss. His hot, wet tongue flicks over my lips, stroking and sucking at them, eliciting a gasp from me.

He takes full advantage of the opportunity and slips his tongue inside my mouth, finding my own and mating with it.

It's the most sensual kiss of my entire life.

One of his large hands moves to the nape of my neck as he tilts my face up to him, granting him deeper access to my mouth.

I move my tongue against his, kissing him back, and a guttural sound tears from his throat. I feel it reverberating through his chest and into my own, and something about it is so raw it makes moisture pool between my thighs.

His hands fist in my hair as he kisses me deeper, hungrier. The kiss is no longer soft and gentle. It's claiming and possessive, and it sends fire rushing throughout my veins.

I'm almost dizzy when he finally pulls back from me and whispers against my lips, "Fuck, sweetheart, you taste like *mine*."

I can't speak. I'm gulping in air like I'm dying, my chest heaving as I stare up at him. A lock of dark hair falls over his forehead, and without thinking, I reach up to brush it back.

It's silky beneath my fingertips, and I watch in wonder as he closes his eyes and turns his head slightly into my touch like a giant cat being stroked. He captures my palm and kisses it, his piercing blue eyes trained on me all the while, and my breath catches in my throat at the look in his.

There is lust in his ocean blue depths, but it's more than that.

He's looking at me with such worship in his eyes.

"Victoria," he says my name again, his eyes blazing down into mine with a promise, "I want you to know before we do this that this is so much more than sex. Once we do this, you become *mine*. In every way. Do you understand what I'm saying to you?"

Maybe his words should frighten me, but they don't. Somehow, they make sense, and they calm me. He's going to take care of me. He's not like the other men who wanted to buy me.

I nod.

"Say it," he prompts me, kissing my palm again.

"Yes," I say, willing to do anything he tells me. I trust him implicitly, which is crazy because I've never really trusted anyone in my entire life.

"Valentine," he prompts me again.

"What?" I shake my head in confusion, still lost in the blue depths of his eyes.

"Say my name. Valentine," he urges me again.

"Valentine," I softly say his name for the first time.

I see the shudder that passes through his entire frame when I say his name. He closes his eyes and draws in a ragged breath. When he reopens then, they're blazing with purpose.

He bends down and scoops me into his arms. My arms instinctively wrap around his neck, and I nuzzle close to him as he carries me over to the bed and lays me gently down on it.

As I wait for him to join me, my eyes flick over to the mirrored windows I can't see out of, and I feel the anxiety creeping back in on me at the thought of all the men sitting on the other side of the window watching us.

"Victoria," Valentine calls my name, and I instantly turn my gaze back to him. He's removed his shirt, revealing the most perfectly defined chest and stomach I've ever seen on a man. I'm trying not to gape, but I can't stop staring at him. Every muscle in his chest and arms and stomach is perfectly defined. They flex and roll beautifully with every movement he makes, and I see the dark hair leading down into a trail into his pants.

Those pants that are sporting the biggest bulge I'eve ever seen in my life.

He's just as huge there as he is everywhere else.

"Eyes on me," he reminds me. "Nothing else exists except us. There's just you and me in this moment."

I nod up at him, too captivated by him to look away.

He begins to kiss all over my face, trailing his way down the side of my throat with gentle sucks and licks that have me tilting my head to give him easier access.

"I knew the first day I saw you, you were going to be mine," he whispers into my ear. "You know I've spent every day since then searching for you? And then here you are...fate intervened to bring us together."

I can't think with his hot breath in my ear, his lips laving my throat, but somewhere in the back of my mind I wonder why *he's* here. Surely, he wasn't here to buy a woman. I just can't see him doing that. And come on, he's so breathtakingly gorgeous he wouldn't have to pay for sex. All he'd have to do is snap his fingers and women would fall at his feet.

I push that thought away. I don't like the thought of him with other women.

"Only us," he whispers to me, as if he can sense the direction my thoughts have taken. He reclaims my lips again in a passionate kiss as his hands continue to slide over me, dancing skillfully over my skin.

"Fuck," he whispers against my mouth, "I want nothing more than to undress you and worship you properly, but I'll be damned if anyone sees another glorious inch of your skin but me. You're for my eyes only, Victoria."

He growls a sound of frustration as he begins kissing his way down my body, over the swell of my breast. He sucks my nipple into his mouth through the thin lace of my bra, and I gasp at the sensation, arching up into him.

"So fucking perfect," he murmurs against my skin as he continues to kiss his way down my stomach and to the area between my thighs.

"I have to taste you," he says reverently as he settles between my legs. He spreads my legs and groans when he sees how wet my panties are. I blush, halfway embarrassed at my body's response, but he grates out, "So fucking wet for me."

The next thing I know I feel his lips on me down *there*. He's kissing me through my panties, and then he pulls them to the side and laves me with his tongue, one long lick from my slit all the way up to my clit.

Sparks are exploding in between my legs, and I jump, but his hands hold me still.

"Fuck, you taste like pure fucking sugar, baby," he says before he begins licking and sucking me ardently, his tongue batting at my clit over and over again.

"Oh god," I can't stop my moans as this incredible pressure builds deep within my core.

Then, I feel his finger pressing into my hole. I'm so wet, it slides in easily, but I still tense at the invasion.

He starts to suck my clit in rhythmic pulses as he moves that finger slowly in and out of me, stretching me and loosening me up.

Oh god, it feels so good. I fist my hands in his hair, half pulling him closer, half pushing him away.

My mind is jumbled. I can't think. All I can do is feel and whine, half sobbing, half begging—for what I don't know.

And then he adds another finger, pushing it inside me and pumping faster while he sucks and swirls his tongue rapidly.

I'm panting, a sheen of sweat breaking out on my skin. My body arches up, reaching for something, and then Valentine groans against my clit, and that does it.

I cry out as white hot lightning crashes through me. I'm pulsing and liquid is flooding between my legs. I vaguely register the sounds of Valentine moaning and lapping it all up, and then the next thing I know he's gathering me up in his arms as he stretches his body protectively over me. He kisses all over my face. "So fucking beautiful when you come for me," he whispers against my cheeks.

I feel the hard rod of his erection pressing against me through his pants, and I boldly move my hand down to cup him.

He hisses in a breath as his wild eyes find mine.

"I can't wait much longer, baby," he grates out from behind clenched teeth.

"Then don't," I tell him, suddenly just as eager to feel him inside me. I feel impossibly connected to this man in a closeness I've never known with another human being before. "Take me," my order comes out breathy, but it's no less effective for that.

It's apparently all he needs to hear because he shucks his pants off in a flash, and then he's covering me with his body again.

He still hasn't removed any of my flimsy clothes. I'm still wearing the thin robe and the lacy bra and panties, and I realize when he pulls my panties to the side like he did when he ate my pussy that he has no intention of undressing me.

"My eyes only," he reaffirms, again as if he's reading my thoughts.

I nod, agreeing with him, grateful that he's unwilling to expose me to all the lecherous, hungry stares I know are hidden behind the glass.

I feel the tip of his cock rubbing against the inside of my thigh. It's wet and leaves a trail of moisture on my skin.

I look up at him and unconsciously lick my lips.

His eyes darken, and he moans before he leans down to kiss me again while he lines himself up with my hole with one hand.

He continues kissing me as he presses the fat tip against me and begins to push.

I gasp into his mouth at the penetration. He feels so much bigger than his fingers did.

"Sshh, it's okay baby," he tries to soothe me, breathing the words against my lips. "I know it's big, and it'll sting a little bit, but I swear to god I'm not going to purposefully hurt you. Just let me in, and I'll make you feel so fucking good, little girl."

I whimper as he continues to press steadily inside me, stretching me.

"Relax, sweetheart," he prompts me.

I try to do as he says. He stops pushing and I look up at him in relief. "It's in?" I ask him, surprised. That wasn't as bad as I thought it'd be.

He doesn't answer. Instead, he leans down and begins kissing and sucking on my neck. I melt underneath his gentle ministrations as he sucks right underneath my ear, causing heat to pool in between my legs.

Then, he suddenly rears back and plows forward, plunging into me. I scream. His mouth crashes down over mine to swallow my cries. He groans a completely primitive sound of male satisfaction and kisses me fiercely as he breaks through my barrier, and then I feel him settle completely inside me.

Oh god, he's impossibly deep, and I feel so stretched. He just holds himself there as he continues to kiss me, coaxing my tongue to dance with his.

My chest is heaving, but the sting is already fading. It's being replaced by a deep ache. My muscles involuntarily clench around him, testing his weight inside me, and he lets out a guttural sound, breaking contact with my lips as he does so.

"Oh fuck, Victoria, baby," he groans into my neck. "You're so fucking tight. Fucking made for my cock, sweetheart." His chest is heaving, and I feel him shudder above me. "I'm not going to last, baby. I've got such a big nut to bust in that tight little pussy. *Fuuuuck...*"

He looks down at me, his expression torn between lust and concern. "Please tell me I didn't hurt you too badly."

I shake my head. "It doesn't hurt anymore." I wiggle beneath him, causing him to slide inside me a bit.

He throws his head back, the muscles in his neck taut, and I moan, "Feels so good."

"Fuck yeah," he says as he begins to move slowly in and out of me.

Every nerve ending in my body is snapping with electricity.

He groans and thrusts deeper and faster within me, his fat tip poking a spot deep inside my womb that sends tingles rushing throughout me.

I moan and arch up into him, seeking out more of the sensation.

"You like that, baby?" he asks directly into my ear as he gathers me tightly in his arms, pressing his body flush against mine and shielding it from the eyes on the other side of the window. He's completely covering me. I'm lost in him.

I wrap my arms and legs around him as I moan my assent.

"Fuck yes, baby, hold on to me. I've got you," he groans out as he begins to pick up speed, hammering into me harder and faster.

He's filling me completely, the slide of him in and out of me causing a delicious friction to build until I'm whimpering, begging him, "Please, please Valentine!"

"Victoria," he rasps out my name as he continues to drive up into me. I feel him swelling within me, getting impossibly bigger and larger, and then he hits that spot one last time, and I shatter, throwing my head back on a moan. I feel my toes curling as every muscle in my body spasms and contracts in a release so intense I feel like I'm leaving my body and floating.

"Oh god, baby," he groans out, his face looking tortured as he feels my pussy pusling around him and gripping him. "I'm right there with you, sweetheart," he says as he pushes up into me again.

"*Fuucck*!" he roars, and then I feel him jerking within me. Hot, wet heat floods inside me. I feel the first spurt splash deep within me in a jet of pressure that makes me climax again. I'm spasming around him as he pulses inside me, flooding me with his seed.

I feel his body go lax above me, though he manages to keep himself propped up on his elbows to keep his weight off me as he keeps my body caged under him, surrounding me with the protective shield of his big shoulders and arms.

Neither of us speaks. There are no words that can truly describe the magnitude of what we just shared.

He's right. That was more than just sex. It's like our souls are now mated together. I feel my spirit wrapped up in his. I'm glowing, and I just want to stay in this cocoon with him forever.

He kisses me again, a kiss full of possession and promise.

And I melt up into him.

Six

Valentine

I'M STILL inside her half hard. Fuck, I want to worship every inch of her body. I didn't get to taste her the way I really want to. I want to lick every inch of her skin, but I'm still very aware of all the lecherous eyes watching us from behind the windows.

They got all the show they're going to get out of us, and I'm sure they were disappointed that I kept her body completely covered by mine the whole time. I didn't remove a scrap of her clothing, though the blood staining the sheets is enough proof that I did indeed take her virginity.

I set her panties back aright, pulling them back to cover her pretty little mound, my mouth already salivating again at the remembered taste of her. Then, I get dressed again myself before I drape my coat back around her shoulders to shield her from prying eyes.

No one will ever look at her again except me.

I lift her into my arms and cradle her against my chest. She doesn't resist. She just wraps her little arms around my neck and burrows deeper into my chest. A surge of protectiveness swells up inside me. I'm undeniably pleased by the way she's clinging to me.

Mine.

"Let's get you home," my voice comes out gruff, but she doesn't seem to mind. No, my little fairy seems to understand what I can't even put into words. Fuck it. We don't even need words. This current runs between us, allowing us to communicate to each other on a soul deep level. I feel her inside me. I never thought I'd be a sucker for that kind of nonsense, but it is what it is.

Victoria and I are undeniably mated with a connection that goes more than skin deep. I felt it that day on the street before I ever even knew her name, but now that I've claimed her as mine, it's only stronger.

As soon as I open the door to leave, we're accosted by Carmichael. "Bravo, Valentine, my man," he's clapping slowly. "Nice show, though I do think the members would have appreciated a bit more of the lady's skin instead of so much of *your* backside."

"Fuck off, Carmichael," I growl at him, the warning clear in my voice. "I played by your rules. Now, we're out of here."

He's glancing at us curiously, though he wisely doesn't say a word.

"Wait," he calls from behind my back as I head for the door with Victoria still clinging to me. I ignore him. We're done here, and I'm not releasing her for anything.

"Valentine," her tiny voice calling my name has me looking down at her tenderly. God, she's so fragile in my arms. My chest tightens at the thought that I could have missed her. She could have been auctioned off to someone else. My arms tighten involuntarily around her at the thought.

"Yes, my love?" I ask her.

Her cheeks turn pink. "I need to use the restroom really quick."

I frown, not wanting to leave her alone even for that, but I walk her over to a restroom and set her on her feet. "I'll be right out here waiting for you," I tell her.

"Okay," she smiles shyly at me before she slips inside and closes the door.

I wait outside the door for what must be at least five minutes before I start to get concerned. I don't want to embarrass her or rush her, but I need to make sure she's okay.

I knock on the door. "Victoria?" I call when there's no answer.

Still no answer. My heart starts to hammer inside my chest. I have a bad feeling. "I'm fixing to bust open this door if you don't answer me by the count of three." I call through the door.

"One..." I begin.

Still no answer.

"Two..." still nothing. A cold sweat breaks out on my brow.

"Three." No sooner do I have the words out of my mouth do I kick open the door, panicking when she's nowhere to be found.

I rush inside, looking everywhere. The space isn't overly large, though it's certainly larger and more opulent than most bathrooms.

And then I see it.

Another door leading into the bathroom. Of all the fucking bathrooms in the place, my dumb ass would take her to some sort of Jack and Jill setup.

I run through the other door, my vision turning red when I realize the danger she's in.

I don't know how I know, but I just fucking *know*

she's in trouble. That the person who was after her before has somehow got her.

"Victoria!" I bellow out her name as I begin tearing through the mansion, hellbent on finding her.

She can't have gotten far. It's only been about five minutes.

I race through the hallways like a mad man, screaming her name, ignoring the stares from all the patrons of this den of iniquity.

I don't know which way I'm running. I'm running blindly, following some instinct that's apparently leading me to her because suddenly I round a corner, and my vision blurs at the sight before me.

Victoria is struggling, her little arms kicking and flailing as a beefy man holds her from behind, his hand clamped down over her mouth to stifle her cries.

"Stop fighting, you little bitch," he snarls at her. "It's not enough that I have to come here and see that you've auctioned off my payment. Now, you think you're going to cheat me entirely? You might not be a virgin anymore, but I don't mind sloppy seconds. I guarantee it's still tight enough that you'll scream when I split you in half with *my* dick."

I don't even remember moving. My blood is pounding in my ears, and I roar as complete and utter rage like I've never known rips through my chest. The next thing I know I feel the satisfying give of the man's nose breaking under my fist. He releases Victoria, and she stumbles back before she bursts into tears and flings herself into my arms.

She's the only thing that saves me from beating him literally to death. Although I itch to keep hitting him, the need to comfort her is stronger, especially when she climbs me like a little monkey and wraps her arms and legs around my front, clinging to me tightly and sobbing into my neck, trembling with obvious fear.

The fucker is writhing on the floor in obvious agony, clutching his nose that's spurting blood. It's too good for him. I wish I'd busted his fucking head wide open.

"Is this him?" I ask her, my voice coming out harsher than I intend, but she realizes the harshness isn't meant for her.

She nods, understanding what I'm asking her, before her voice comes out tremulously, finally explaining, "Yes, he's my landlord. When I couldn't pay my rent, he..." she stumbles over her words, her chin trembling before she manages to get it out, "he demanded my virginity as payment..."

She trails off, and I finish her sentence for her. "So you decided you might as well auction it off and get paid more for your trouble so you'd never find yourself in that situation again."

She nods weakly, looking ashamed.

"Hey," I raise her chin to me and make her meet my eyes. "You have nothing to be ashamed of. You were trapped, and you didn't know what to do, but nothing like that is ever going to happen to you again," I vow to her. And I fucking mean it. Nothing is ever going to touch this girl again. Over my dead body, and even from the grave, I'll do everything within my power to protect her. Raise hell from beneath the earth and haunt every motherfucker who would come near her.

"Valentine," she bites her lip nervously, obviously troubled by something. Whatever it is, I swear to god, I'll hunt it down and obliterate it.

"What is it, sweetheart?" I prompt her.

"Why were you here tonight?"

Ah, so that's what's bothering her. Her little brow is furrowed, but she's looking up at me with wide, trusting eyes like I must have a good explanation for being in a place like this. And I do.

I relax and pull her closer to me. "I was lured here for a supposed business meeting. I had no fucking idea what would be going on here tonight, but thank fuck I was here, baby."

I pull her closer to me and place a kiss in her hair.

"You were pulled here to rescue me." She voices what we're both thinking, what we're both feeling.

I just nod, silently agreeing with her.

"What the fuck, Valentine?" Carmichael finally bursts onto the scene. "What's all the yelling for—" he comes to an abrupt stop when he sees the fucker still down on the floor.

"This is your fucking mess," I tell him disdainfully, Victoria still clutched against me. I'm holding her with one hand around her back and the other under her sweet ass, holding her up.

"You're goddamned lucky she wasn't harmed by the bastard. Otherwise, it'd be more than *your* nose I broke." I'm flaming fucking mad at this entire situation and the fact that Carmichael is sleazy enough to be involved in something like this.

Carmichael's face pales, and his jaw tightens. He knows I mean business.

I start walking for the door.

"Wait," he dares to say. "Where are you going with her? We have to make sure she gets her cut of the pay."

Victoria pulls back from me far enough to turn her head and look directly at Carmichael, the ice in her eyes enough to chill to the bone. "Fuck you," she says.

I stroke her back reassuringly, proud as fuck of her for standing up for herself, before I turn her back around to me and kiss her thoroughly.

My beautiful, brave girl.

"Take me wherever you go," she breathes against my lips when we finally break the kiss.

So I do.

I take her home with me and take her all over again, worshipping her fully naked body the way I wanted to for her first time.

Afterward, as she's laying on my chest and I'm running my fingers through her hair, she muses, "Who would have thought I'd lose my V-card in a V-Day auction on Valentine's Day to my Valentine?"

I grin down at her when she strings it all together that way. "You're the best little Valentine I've ever had," I tell her, stroking my hand down her cheek, marveling at her perfection. God, I can't stop touching her.

"Have you had many?" she blinks up at me.

"Actually, no. I've never had one at all," I tell her honestly. I've never been with a woman on Valentine's Day before. It just never worked out where I was in a relationship on the commercial holiday.

She smiles then. "Me either."

"You better not have been," I growl, tightening my arms around her, jealous at just the thought of anyone else having even kissed her. "You're all mine."

"All yours," she repeats with another beautiful smile. Fuck, I could just watch her smile all day and be completely content with that.

"I hope you know I'm never letting you go," I growl at her, my voice gravelly with my sudden emotion. I'm dead serious. This woman is everything to me. She's mine. Forever.

"You only paid for my virginity," she points out teasingly with an arched brow.

I flip her over so my body is on top of hers, pinning her down. She smirks up at me, the little minx.

I kiss and suck at her neck, marking her as mine. A deep sense of satisfaction settles over me when I pull back and see my mark on her skin. "No way, baby. I'm keeping you. I bought you for life."

"Then take me. Keep me," she says breathily.

So I do.

Epilogue

Three Years Later

Victoria

I SMILE to myself when I think of what Valentine's reaction to what I'm wearing under my little red dress is going to be.

It's Valentine's Day, our two-year anniversary—well, though we've been married two years, we've been together for three, so I guess really it's our three-year anniversary.

In any case, I'm looking forward to driving my husband crazy.

He loves me in white underthings, maybe because that's what I'd been wearing our first time, but I've never worn something quite like this before.

He bought me on Valentine's Day at the V-Day auction. He took my virginity and made me his that day. Then, we got married a year later on Valentine's Day.

Yeah, V-Day is kind of our special day.

We haven't had any children yet, though that's certainly not for lack of trying. Valentine would fuck me all day every day if he still didn't have his business to run, and I didn't have mine.

I smile a secret smile to myself when I think of the second part of my Valentine's Day present to him.

True to his word, he did the deal with Carmichael, but as soon as their contract was up, he kicked him to the curb and hasn't dealt with him since.

Instead, my husband funded my business venture. It's something that's dear to my heart. I never wanted another woman to find herself in the desperate situation I was in, so I started my own women's shelter. It's a place for women who are down on their luck and need somewhere to stay while they get back on their feet so they don't have to resort to selling their bodies—or virginity —off to scumbags just to make ends meet.

Of course, I wouldn't change anything about my past. It's how I met my Valentine, after all. But even if he hadn't saved me from making a terrible mistake at the auction, I truly believe we'd have found each other because he's right. We're soulmates, and our hearts would have drifted together no matter what.

Fate would have brought us together.

I walk out onto the balcony, and my heart melts at the display before me.

He's gone all out. The entire space is lit with rose-scented candles. I can smell the intoxicating fragrance wrapping around me. Rose petals are scattered all over the white tablecloth and the balcony. Champagne is chilling on ice.

And he's standing there, looking breathtakingly handsome in his custom suit, though he's set the jacket aside, and his sleeves are rolled up to reveal his forearms.

God, I never would have thought I would have a kink for a man's arms, but my husband's are to die for. I have a thing for everything about him.

"There she is," he says as he starts walking toward me, the appreciation in his eyes evident as he sweeps over my form. God, I'll never tire of seeing the love and adoration in his eyes as he gazes at me like this. "My beautiful little wife."

"My handsome husband," I answer him back and tilt my head up to accept his kiss.

He wastes no time in parting my lips and kissing me

hungrily, devouring my mouth and leaving me trembling in the wake of his kiss.

He breaks off long enough for us breathe. We're both shaken by the kiss, our foreheads pressed together as we struggle for breath.

He finally groans, "Fuck it," before he hoists me into his arms.

I wrap my legs around his waist and hold on to him, everything else forgotten in the wake of our sudden desire for one another. I hear him unzipping his pants, and he groans as his cock springs free.

Moisture floods my pussy in response, and I can already feel my clit throbbing in anticipation. It's always like this with us, our response to one another immediate.

We're so in tune it's like we're one person even when we aren't joined in this most primal way.

Valentine's fingers slide under my dress to pull aside my panties, and then he stills when he meets my bare, wet pussy instead. He pulls back and looks at me with wide, lust-filled eyes.

I bite my lip, half crazed with lust myself as I feel his fingers press more firmly against me.

He pulls back and looks down, letting out a curse when his suspicions are confirmed.

I'm wearing white, lacy crotchless panties.

"You like?" I ask him, my voice coming out husky.

"I fucking love," he growls out before he begins to stroke my clit rapidly. "You know exactly how to drive me fucking crazy, don't you, baby?"

I'm not given a chance to answer because his lips crash down onto mine in a bruising, claiming kiss just as he thrusts up into me in one swift movement.

I cry out into his mouth as I clutch him tighter about the neck.

He groans and moves his lips over to my neck to lick and suck, refreshing his mark. Valentine likes to keep my neck marked, and I'm totally okay with that. I love his possessiveness. I love seeing his marks on me and knowing that I'm totally claimed by my soulmate.

He pumps up into me, hitting that spot within me just right, and my head falls back on a deep moan. "Oh god, Valentine!"

"Fuck, I can't get enough of you, Victoria," he groans in my ear. "I need to feel that little pussy falling open all over my cock every second of the goddamned day."

"Yes," I moan against him as I push myself down onto him, meeting him thrust for thrust, causing him to go even deeper.

His breath hitches, and then he curses, "Fuck, woman, you're going to have me nutting in no time."

"Yes!" I moan again, his dirty talk turning me on

even more. I love when he loses control and speaks filth to me while he's fucking me.

He knows it too. "I'm gonna nut so much in you there's no way you won't get fucking pregnant this time, sweetheart," he's panting, a feral sound as he continues to hammer his big dick up inside me, deliciously stretching me until I'm delirious with pleasure. "You want that? You want me to breed you?" His own eyes are crazed. I know he's close. I can feel him swelling inside me.

"Oh fuck, yes!" I cry out as one last jab sends me flying over the precipice. Heat soars through my veins as I come, spasming around him.

He feels it, and that sets him off. "Oh fuck! Oh fuck, Victoria!" he groans. "Here comes that big nut just for you baby! Ugh!" He moans loudly, and I feel him jerking inside me as he releases his seed into me. It fills me completely and overflows, coating my thighs and dripping down over his balls.

We're a glorious, sticky mess, and I go limp in his arms.

Still holding himself inside me, he sits us down so that I'm straddling him.

I kiss him lazily. He hums a sound of approval and I feel him harden inside me, but I pull back before he gets too worked up again. I have news for him. "That was amazing, babe, but I'm afraid you won't be able to get me pregnant."

His brow furrows, and concern lights in his eyes.

Before he can jump to conclusions and start freaking out and thinking that something's wrong, I rush to add, "Because I'm already pregnant, Valentine."

He goes completely still beneath me. His blue eyes are wide as they flick between mine, and then a huge grin breaks out on his face. "You're pregnant, honey?"

I nod, my own grin matching his own. "Happy Valentine's Day," I tell him, elation overtaking me at the complete happiness I see on his face.

He laughs, a completely joyous sound as he crushes me to him, hugging me tightly and kissing me with all the love that flows between us.

"I love you so fucking much, my Victoria," his voice is raspy with emotion, and it makes my heart swell with love for him.

"I love you too, my Valentine."

Connect with Emma!

Visit Emma's website to get a FREE book you can't get anywhere else: www.authoremmabray.com.

Want more another quick romance by Emma Bray?
Keep reading for an excerpt from Secrets.

Chapter 1

Zane

My name is Zane Culvert, and I have a secret. Well, two secrets, actually.

My first secret?

I know all of Anne Johnson's secrets.

I know that her mother sent her to kindergarten a year early just to get her out of her hair while she fucked the johns that paid her rent.

I know that because of that, Anne was always the youngest and smallest one in her class and that she always felt left behind and mostly stuck to herself throughout grade school.

I know that she threw herself into her studies, graduated early, and started attending college at seventeen instead of eighteen, hence why she's the youngest fully licensed elementary school teacher in the city.

I know that she's really the face behind Charlotte Locke, the famed naughty romance novelist.

I know that despite her erotic writings, Anne is really a virgin.

Thank God for that. Really, it saves me a lot of time and aggravation. I don't have a list of men to kill now. She really did the world a service by retaining her innocence.

I know that she still feels guilty about her mother's death. It wasn't her fault at all, but she feels like she should have done more, sat with her more in the hospital as the cancer at away at her body.

That's natural guilt, I suppose. When someone you love dies, you'll always feel like you didn't do enough, like there was more you could have done—no matter how much you did.

That's what I've heard anyway. I don't know from firsthand experience seeing as how I've never cared for anyone enough to care when they died.

One of my many character flaws, I suppose. A lack of empathy, the psychologists had called it.

Makes me perfect for working the unsavory jobs I do on the streets, dealing with the dregs of society.

But the nature of my work isn't my second secret.

No, my second secret?

My second secret is this: Anne Johnson is my obsession. I watch her every second of the motherfucking day.

I've been watching her for two years now. I suppose "stalking" is the technical term for what I'm doing, but I don't like to call it that.

Stalking sounds so...devious, calculated.

And while I am those things—and frequently—that's not the case when I watch Anne.

When I watch Anne, I *feel*.

I feel so many things. Despair, desire, lust, pain, anxiety, fear. I feel more than I've ever felt in my pitiful excuse for an existence.

She gives me a reason to exist. Watching her, protecting her, guarding her from afar. She is my purpose in this life.

Anne Johnson is my everything.

And she doesn't even know it.

I've thought of approaching her many times. God knows how much I long to take her in my arms, hold her against me, run my fingers through her auburn hair and along her milky white skin just to see if she's as soft as she looks.

I want to cherish her, see her smile, be the cause of her smile, feel her light shining down on me. Have her blue eyes peering up at me behind those tortoiseshell cat-eye glasses she wears.

I would die of happiness at just one look from her.

This feeling that grips my chest and tightens it every time I think of her—much less look at her...

I don't know what to call it. I've determined that it must be "love." Something I never thought myself capable of feeling. I'm still not entirely sure I'm capable of it.

And there are so many definitions of it, depending upon who you ask. All I know is that I feel like I'll die if I don't see her every day, that I'd give my life to protect her.

I'm perfectly content to sit and watch her sleeping for hours.

I've got cameras rigged up all throughout her apartment. I have a tracking device on her phone. I frequently sneak into her apartment and read her diary, catching up on all the thoughts in my beautiful little Annie's head.

That's what I call her secretly.

My little Annie.

There's nothing I'd rather read than her innermost thoughts. Some might call me breaking into her apartment, reading her diary, and keeping tabs on her everywhere she goes an invasion of privacy, but I can't help it. Everything about her fascinates me.

I feel closer to her than anyone else on this entire planet.

And she doesn't even know I exist.

I stroke my finger over her face on my phone screen where I have my live camera feed of her pulled up.

She's curled up on her side, her hands in little balls under her chin as she slumbers peacefully.

Like a pretty little kitten.

Want more Emma Bray? Go to www.authoremmabray.com.

* 9 7 9 8 2 1 5 1 0 0 3 8 7 *